MOBY DICK

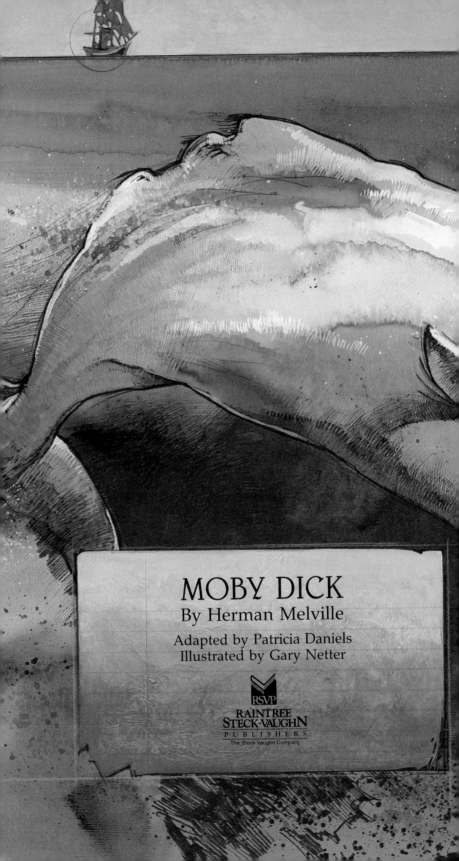

MOBY DICK
By Herman Melville

Adapted by Patricia Daniels
Illustrated by Gary Netter

RSVP

RAINTREE
STECK-VAUGHN
P U B L I S H E R S
The Steck-Vaughn Company

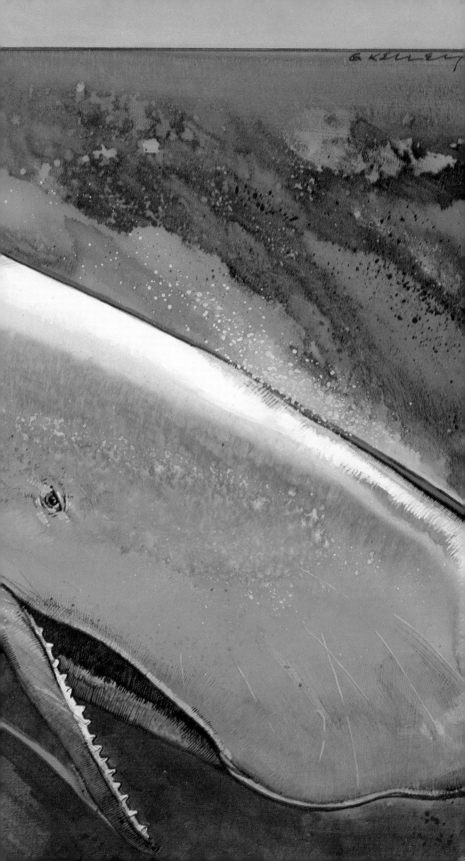

Library of Congress Number: 81-15386

Library of Congress Cataloging-in-Publication Data

Daniels, Patricia.
  Moby Dick, or The white whale.

  SUMMARY: A young seaman joins the crew of the whaling ship Pequod, led by the fanatical Captain Ahab in pursuit of the white whale Moby Dick.
  [1. Whaling—Fiction. 2. Whales—Fiction 3. Sea stories]
I. Kelley, Gary, ill. II. Melville, Herman, 1819-1891. Moby Dick. III.Title.
PZ7.D2195Mo   [Fic.]   81-15386

ISBN 0-8172-1679-0 hardcover library binding

ISBN 0-8114-6834-8 softcover binding

14 15 16 17 18 19 20   99 98 97 96 95 94

CONTENTS

CHAPTER ONE

Call me Ishmael. Some years ago, having little or no money in my purse, and nothing to interest me on shore, I thought I would sail about a little and see the watery part of the world. Whenever I find myself growing grim about the mouth; whenever it is a damp, drizzly November in my soul — then, I get to the sea as soon as I can.

I do not mean that I ever go to sea as a passenger. No, I always go as a sailor, because they pay me for my trouble, whereas they never pay passengers a single penny that I ever heard of. But whereas I had repeatedly smelt the sea as a merchant sailor, I now took it into my head to go on a whaling voyage.

Chief among my reasons was the idea of the great whale himself. Such a mysterious monster roused all my curiosity. Then, too, I love to sail forbidden seas and land on strange coasts. And so it was that I stuffed a shirt or two into my old carpet-bag, tucked it under my arm, and started for Cape Horn and the Pacific.

I arrived in New Bedford on a Saturday night in December. There I was disappointed to learn that the little packet for Nantucket had sailed, and that the next was not till the following Monday. For my mind was made up to sail in no other than a Nantucket craft. Though New Bedford has gradually been taking over the business of whaling, Nantucket was the great original — the place where the first dead American whale was stranded.

Now, having two nights to spend in New Bedford, I

must find a place to eat and sleep. It was a dark and dismal night, and with halting steps I paced the streets. At last I came to a dim sort of light, and heard a forlorn creaking in the air. Looking up, I saw a swinging sign over the door with a white painting on it, showing a tall straight jet of misty spray. These words were underneath — "The Spouter-Inn: — Peter Coffin."

Coffin? — Spouter? — Rather ominous, I thought. But it is a common name in Nantucket, they say. So I scraped the ice from my feet and entered. It was a dusky place, with low beams and old wrinkled planks. Projecting from the corner of the room was the vast arched bone of a whale's jaw, so wide a coach might almost drive beneath it. And within these jaws were shelves and bottles, and a little withered old man, like another cursed Jonah, who sold the sailors their drinks. I sought the landlord, and was told that his house was full — not a room to be had. "But avast," he added, tapping his forehead, " you hain't no objections to sharing a harpooneer's blanket, have ye? I s'pose you are goin' a whalin', so you'd better get used to that sort of thing."

I told him that I never liked to sleep two in a bed; that if I should ever do so, it would depend upon who the harpooneer might be, and that if he (the landlord) really had no other place for me, I would put up with the half of any decent man's blanket.

I ate a dinner of dumplings and observed a wild set of sailors that had rolled in. In their shaggy watch coats, with their beards stiff with icicles, they seemed an eruption of bears from Labrador. As I watched them I formed a plan. No man likes to sleep two in a bed — and the more I thought of this harpooneer, the more I hated the thought of sleeping with him. It was fair to presume that as a harpooneer, his linen would not be the finest. I began to twitch all over. Besides, it was getting late — why wasn't this decent man home by now?

"Landlord! I've changed my mind about that harpooneer — I shan't sleep with him. I'll try the bench here."

"Just as you please," he said. But I found that the bench was a foot too narrow, and a foot too short.

I began to think that after all I might be too prejudiced against this unknown harpooneer. Thinks I, I'll wait awhile, and have a good look at him. But time passed, and there was no sign of him.

"Landlord!" said I, "what sort of a chap is he — does he always keep such late hours?"

The landlord chuckled. "No," he answered, "generally he's an early bird. But tonight he went out a-peddling, and maybe he can't sell his head."

"Can't sell his head? What sort of a bamboozling story is this you are telling me?"

"Be easy, be easy," the landlord said. "This harpooneer has just arrived from the South Seas, where he bought up a lot of 'balmed New Zealand heads, and he's sold all of 'em but one."

This account cleared up the mystery. At the same time, what could I think of a harpooneer who stayed out of a Saturday night, engaged in such a cannibal business? Nevertheless, I was shown into my small room. In it were a huge bed, a large seaman's bag, holding the harpooneer's clothes, and a tall harpoon standing at the head of the bed. I made no more ado, but tumbled into bed.

I was just sliding into sleep when I heard a heavy footfall in the passage. Lord save me, thinks I, that must be the harpooneer. I lay perfectly still as the stranger entered the room and placed his candle on the floor in a corner. When he turned around — good heavens! What a sight! His face was of a dark, purplish yellow color, here and there stuck over with large, blackish squares. At first I thought he must have been in a fight; but then I saw that the squares must be tattoos. Then he took off his hat, and I came nigh singing out with fresh surprise. There was no hair on his head — nothing but a small scalp-knot twisted upon his forehead. His bald purplish head looked for all the world

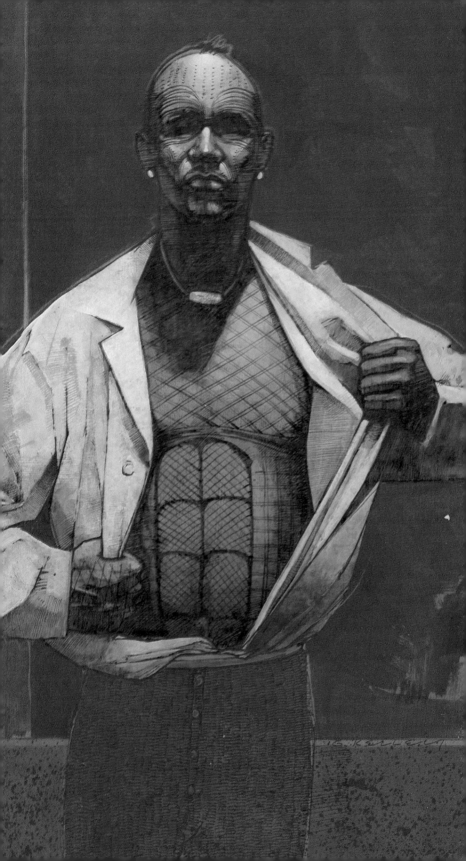

like a mildewed skull. Meanwhile, he continued undressing, and I saw that his chest and arms were checkered with the same squares as his face. Still more, his very legs were marked, as if a parcel of dark green frogs were running up the trunks of young palms. It was now quite plain that he must be some abominable savage shipped aboard of a whaleman in the South Seas.

I thought I should speak up, but before I knew what to say, this wild cannibal sprang into bed with me. I cried out, I could not help it now; and he gave a sudden grunt of astonishment.

"Who-e debel you?" he said. "You no speak-e, I kill-e."

"Landlord! Peter Coffin!" shouted I. "Landlord! Coffin! Save me!"

The landlord came into the room, light in hand, and leaping from the bed I ran up to him.

"Don't be afraid now," said he, grinning. "Queequeg here wouldn't harm a hair of your head."

"Stop your grinning," shouted I, "and why didn't you tell me that that infernal harpooneer was a cannibal?"

"I thought ye know'd it; didn't I tell ye, he was a-peddlin' heads around town? Queequeg, look here — this man sleep-e you — you sabbee?"

"Me sabbee plenty," grunted Queequeg. "You gettee in," he added, throwing the bedclothes to one side. I stood looking at him a moment. For all his tattooings he was on the whole a clean, comely looking cannibal. What's all this fuss I have been making, thought I — the man's a human being just as I am. He has just as much reason to fear me, as I have to be afraid of him. Better to sleep with a sober cannibal than a drunken Christian. I turned in, and never slept better in my life.

After this Queequeg and I became regular friends. Savage though he was, his face had something in it which was not disagreeable. You cannot hide the soul. In his deep eyes and lofty bearing there seemed tokens of a spirit that would dare a thousand devils.

He seemed to take to me as naturally as I to him. He told me he was a native of Kokovoko, an island not down in any map; true places never are. His father was a high chief, but Queequeg gave up all that to go to sea with Christians and learn their ways. They had made a harpooneer out of him; when he knew I intended to sail out of Nantucket, he at once resolved to sail with me.

On Monday we boarded a little schooner for Nantucket, and on the next day I walked out among the shipping. Queequeg had consulted his little god Yojo that he carried with him everywhere, and Yojo had told him that I should select our craft. I learned that there were three ships up for three-years' voyages — the *Devil-Dam,* the *Tit-bit,* and the *Pequod.* When I looked around the *Pequod,* I decided that this was the very ship for us.

She was a quaint old craft, decorated all around with her trophies. Her open bulwarks were like one huge jaw, with pins made of the long sharp teeth of the sperm whale. The tiller was in one piece, strangely carved, and made from the long narrow lower jaw of her ancient foe. A noble craft, but somehow sad. All noble things are touched with that.

On the quarter-deck I spied a brown and burly seaman.

"Is this the captain of the *Pequod?*" said I, walking up to him.

"Supposing it is, what dost thou want of him?" he demanded.

"I was thinking of shipping."

"Why? What takes thee a-whaling? I want to know that before I think of shipping ye."

"Well, sir, I want to see what whaling is. I want to see the world."

"Want to see what whaling is, eh? Have ye clapped eye on Captain Ahab?"

"Who is Captain Ahab, sir?"

"Captain Ahab is the captain of this ship."

"I am mistaken then. I thought I was speaking to the captain," I said.

"Thou art speaking to Captain Peleg. It belongs to me and Captain Bildad to see the *Pequod* fitted out for the voyage. We are part owners. But, if thou wantest to know what whaling is, clap an eye on Captain Ahab, young man. Thou wilt find that he has only one leg."

"What do you mean, sir? Was the other one lost by a whale?"

"Young man, come closer to me: it was devoured, chewed up, crunched by the monstrousest whale that ever chipped a boat!"

I was a little alarmed, but eventually convinced Captain Peleg and his companion Captain Bildad of my desire to go a-whaling. As they brought forth my papers, I said, "Captain Peleg, I have a friend with me who wants to ship too. Shall I bring him down tomorrow?"

"Has he ever whaled any?" he asked.

"Killed more whales than I can count."

"Well, bring him along then."

I turned to go, and then thought that the captain with whom I was to sail remained unseen. Turning back, I asked Captain Peleg where Captain Ahab was to be found.

"Oh, ye won't be able to see Captain Ahab; he keeps close inside the house. He's a queer man, Captain Ahab, but a good one; thou'lt like him well enough. He's a grand, ungodly, god-like man! Mark ye — he's Ahab, boy, and Ahab of old, thou knowest, was a crowned king."

"And an evil one. When that wicked king was slain, the dogs, did they not lick his blood?"

"Look ye, lad," said Peleg, with a strange look in his eye, "never say that on board the *Pequod*. Captain Ahab did not name himself. He's a good man; moody, perhaps, and savage sometimes, since he lost his leg by that accursed whale; but that will all pass off. So good-bye to thee, and wrong not Captain Ahab because he happens to have a wicked name."

And so I walked away, full of thoughtfulness.

CHAPTER TWO

As Queequeg and I walked up to the *Pequod* the next morning, we heard a voice from the deck. Captain Peleg shouted that he had not suspected my friend was a cannibal. He let no cannibals on board, he said, unless they showed their papers.

"I say," said Peleg, "tell — what's his name? — tell Quohog there to step along. By the great anchor, what a harpoon he's got there! And he handles it about right. I say, Quohog, did you ever stand in the head of a whaleboat? Did you ever strike a fish?"

Without saying a word, Queequeg jumped upon the boat and held up his harpoon.

"Captain," he cried, "you see him small drop tar on water dere? Spose him one whale eye, den!" And taking aim at it, he darted the iron clear across the ship's deck, and struck the tar spot out of sight.

"Now," said Queequeg, "spose him one whale eye. Why, dad whale dead."

"Quick, Bildad," said Peleg, "get the ship's papers. We must have Hedgehog, I mean Quohog, in one of our boats!"

So down we went into the cabin, and to my great joy Queequeg soon belonged to the same ship's company that I did.

"Shipmates, have ye shipped in that ship?"

Queequeg and I had just left the *Pequod,* when those words were put to us by a shabby stranger.

"Yes," said I, "we have just signed the papers."

"Anything down there about your souls?"

"What are you jabbering about, shipmate?"

"Ye haven't seen Captain Ahab yet, have ye?"

"What do you know about him?" I asked.

"They didn't tell ye about that thing that happened to him off Cape Horn, long ago? Nothing about the deadly fight with the Spaniard in the church in Santa? And nothing about losing his leg last voyage, according to the prophecy?"

"My friend," said I, "let me tell you, I know all about the loss of his leg."

"*All* about it, eh? Sure you do? Well, what's signed, is signed; what's to be, will be. Morning to ye, shipmates. I'm sorry I stopped ye."

"Morning it is," said I. "But stop, tell me your name, will you?"

"Elijah."

Elijah! thought I. The biblical prophet! As Queequeg and I walked back to the inn, he seemed to be following us. Finally, though, he passed by without noticing us; and I forgot about him.

In a few days the *Pequod* was ready to sail. Queequeg and I arrived at the ship before dawn, and sat down to watch the other sailors come aboard in twos and threes. Towards noon the ship began to move out; Peleg and Bildad were to pilot her out to sea, and then they would leave and return to port. Peleg moved along the deck and swore in the most frightful way. When I paused for a moment in my work, I felt a sudden sharp poke in my rear, and turned to see Captain Peleg withdrawing his leg. That was my first kick.

"Spring, thou sheep-head!" he roared, and turned to Queequeg. "Spring, Quohog!"

It came time for Bildad and Peleg to depart; Captain Ahab was still nowhere to be seen. They lingered to the last moment, then dropped into the small boat that would take them back to land. A cold, damp night breeze was blowing, and a screaming gull flew overhead. We gave three heavy-hearted cheers, and blindly plunged like fate into the long Atlantic.

The chief mate of the *Pequod* was Starbuck, a native of Nantucket, and a Quaker. He was a thin, dry, serious man, but a strong one. He seemed able to endure anything from Polar snow to burning sun. Looking into his eyes, you seemed to see the images of the thousand dangers he had calmly faced in life.

Yet, for all his strength, he had a deep natural awe of the sea. "I will have no man in my boat," said Starbuck, "who is not afraid of a whale." He knew that a fearless man is a more dangerous comrade than a coward.

Stubb was the second mate. He was a native of Cape Cod, and a happy-go-lucky man. Good-humored and careless, he ran his whale-boat as if the most deadly meeting with a whale were a dinner, and the crew his invited guests. Long habit had, for Stubb, changed the jaws of death into an easy chair.

The third mate was Flask, from Martha's Vineyard. He was a short, stout fellow, who seemed to think that whales had personally affronted him. Therefore it was a point of honor with him to destroy them whenever met. In his opinion, the great whale was but a kind of large mouse, needing only a little time and trouble in order to kill and boil.

These three mates — Starbuck, Stubb, and Flask — commanded three of the *Pequod's* boats as headsmen. With each mate went a harpooneer; Queequeg became Starbuck's harpooneer.

For several days after we left Nantucket, nothing was seen of Captain Ahab. Then, as I reached the deck one gray and gloomy morning, cold shivers ran over me. Captain Ahab stood upon his quarter-deck.

He was a high, broad, solid man. There seemed no sign of illness about him. Rather, he looked like a man cut away

from the stake, when the fire has run over his body without burning it. Threading its way out from his gray hairs, and running down one side of his brown face and neck until it disappeared in his clothing, was a bright white mark. Whether that mark was born with him, or whether it was a scar, no one could say.

So grim did this look, that for a few moments I hardly noted the white leg upon which he partly stood. A hole had been cut on each side of the quarter-deck and his bone leg fit into that hole; Captain Ahab stood straight, and looked out at the water. There was a firm will in that look. Not a word did he say, nor did his mates speak to him.

After that, he came on deck every day. As the weather warmed, even Ahab seemed to welcome the pleasant air. More than once he had a look which in any other man would have been a smile.

CHAPTER THREE

It was during this pleasant weather that my first mast-head came round.

To man the mast-head means to climb up a mast a hundred feet or so, to stand upon two thin sticks called the cross-trees. Here, tossed about by the sea, the beginner feels about as cozy as he would standing on a bull's horns. Nevertheless, in calm weather it is delightful. There you stand, striding along the deep, as if the masts were gigantic stilts.

The purpose of the mast-head is to keep a look-out for whales. I must say I kept but sorry guard. Lulled by the rolling ship, with the problem of the universe to think of, how could I follow the order, "Keep your weather eye open, and sing out every time."

One morning, about this time, Ahab came out on deck and began to pace. He was full of intense thought.

"Do ye see him, Flask?" whispered Stubb. "Something pecks at him. 'Twill soon be out."

The hours wore on, and still Ahab paced. It drew near the close of day. Suddenly he came to a halt, and ordered Starbuck to send everybody aft.

"Sir!" said the mate, surprised. This order is seldom given on ship-board.

"Send everybody aft," repeated Ahab. "Mast-heads, there! Come down!"

When all were assembled, he began to pace again. His face looked like the sea when a storm is coming up. But this did not last long. Pausing, he cried:

"What do ye do when ye see a whale, men?"

"Sing out for him!" was the reply.

"Good!" cried Ahab. "And what do ye do next, men?"

"Lower away, and after him!"

"And what tune is it ye pull to, men?"

"A dead whale or a stove boat!"

Ahab's face grew more glad at every shout. He spoke thus:

"All ye mast-headers have heard me give orders about a white whale? Look ye! Do ye see this Spanish ounce of gold?" He held up a bright coin to the sun. "It is a sixteen dollar piece, men. Do ye see it? Mr. Starbuck, hand me that hammer."

He walked toward the main-mast with the hammer lifted up in one hand, and the gold coin in the other. He cried, "Whoever of ye raises me a white-headed whale with a wrinkled brow and a crooked jaw — whoever of ye raises that same white whale, he shall have this gold coin!"

"Hurrah!" cried the seamen as Ahab nailed the coin to the mast.

"It's a white whale, I say," continued Ahab. "Skin your eyes for him, men. Look sharp for white water."

"Captain Ahab," said a harpooneer, "that white whale must be the same that some call Moby Dick."

"Aye, men!" cried Ahab. "It is Moby Dick — Moby Dick — Moby Dick!"

"Captain Ahab," said Starbuck. "Captain Ahab, I have heard of Moby Dick. Was it not Moby Dick that took off thy leg?"

"Who told thee that?" cried Ahab. "Aye, Starbuck, it was Moby Dick that dismasted me. Aye, aye! It was that accursed White Whale!" Then tossing both arms he cried out: "Aye, and I'll chase him round Good Hope, and round the Horn, and round the Norway Maelstrom before I give him up. And this is what ye have shipped for, men! To chase the White Whale over all sides of the earth. What say ye, men? I think ye do look brave."

"Aye, aye!" shouted the seamen.

"God bless ye," Ahab said. "But what's this long face about, Mr. Starbuck? Wilt thou not chase the White Whale? Art not game for Moby Dick?"

"I am game for his crooked jaw, Captain Ahab, if it fairly comes in the way of the business we follow. But I came here to hunt whales, not my captain's revenge. Revenge on a dumb animal," he cried, "that simply struck thee from blindest instinct! To be angered with a dumb thing, Captain Ahab, seems insulting to God — blasphemy."

"Hark ye," said Ahab. "Talk not to me of blasphemy, man. I'd strike the sun if it insulted me. And surely this is no great task for Starbuck. Will the best lance in all Nantucket hang back from this one hunt?"

"God keep us all!" said Starbuck, but he said no more.

I, Ishmael, was one of that crew; my shouts had gone up with theirs. A wild feeling was in me — Ahab's deathless feud seemed mine. With greedy ears I learned the history of the White Whale.

Only a few fishermen had actually seen this monster and given chase. Whalers were scattered around the world. From time to time a boat would report meeting a whale of uncommon size and evil nature. Such a whale, after doing great harm to the fishermen, had completely escaped them. In the beginning whalers had lowered their boats for him as they would have done for any other whale. But at length, so many hunters were hurt and killed that the courage of these brave men was badly shaken. So many stories began to spread about the White Whale that he began to seem more than just a whale.

It began to be suggested that Moby Dick was everywhere — that he had actually been seen in different parts of the world at the same time. Nor was this idea without some reason. No one understands the secrets of sea currents, nor the hidden ways of the sperm whale. No one can say how whales travel so quickly and widely as they do.

Nevertheless, some whalemen went still further in speaking of Moby Dick. They claimed he was immortal; that groves of spears could be planted in his flanks, and he would still swim away unharmed. But even without these strange ideas, there was enough in the earthly form of the monster to strike the mind. It was not just his size that marked him. He had a strange snow-white wrinkled forehead and a high white hump. These features marked him, even at a distance.

More than all, his treacherous retreats struck fear into whalemen. For, when swimming from his hunters with every appearance of alarm, he had many times been known to turn around and break their boats to splinters.

Just such a thing had happened to Ahab. Since the time the monster took his leg off, he hated it. All evil, to crazy Ahab, was given life in Moby Dick.

CHAPTER FOUR

It was a hot, cloudy afternoon. Queequeg and I were sitting on deck, weaving a mat, when we heard a cry from the mast-head.

"There she blows! There, there she blows!"

"Where away?"

"On the lee beam, about two miles away! A school of them!"

Instantly all was noise and movement. The crews of the ship's boats ran to the rail of the *Pequod*, and Ahab appeared on deck.

"Lower away!" he shouted. "Lower away there, I say."

The men sprang over the rail, and released the three boats into the sea. Then the sailors leaped goat-like into the tossed boats below. In a fourth boat was Ahab. The boats pulled out across the waves.

"Spread yourselves," cried Ahab. "Pull out!"

"Pull, my children, pull my little ones," sighed Stubb to his crew. "Softly, softly! That's it! Stop snoring, ye sleepers, and pull!"

Ahab and each of the mates held the steering oar at the stern (back end) of each boat. The crew strained at the oars, while a harpooneer sat in a raised box in the bow (front end). Ahab threw out his arm, and instantly the boats paused. The whales had settled down into the blue.

"Thou, Queequeg, stand up!" cried Starbuck.

The savage sprang up and gazed out toward the spot where the whales had last been seen. On his platform at the stern of the boat Starbuck likewise stood up. Then a harpooneer cried out:

"There they are!"

To a landsman no whales would have been seen. But ahead there were spouts of vapor above a troubled bit of white water.

The boats tore after that one spot of troubled water and air. It was a sight full of quick wonder and awe! The great waves made a hollow roar as they rolled past the four boats. Each boat would tip for an instant on the knifelike edge of a sharp wave. Then it would dip into a watery valley with a head-long, sledlike slide. Behind the boats was the wondrous sight of the ivory *Pequod* bearing down with outstretched sails, like a wild hen after her screaming brood. The sky was growing dark as a storm began to brew, but we set our sails in the small boats and rushed toward the dancing white water.

"Give way, men," whispered Starbuck, "there's time to kill a fish yet before the storm comes. Stand up, Queequeg! That's his hump. *There*, give it to him!"

A rushing sound leaped out of the boat. It was Queequeg's harpoon. Then all was confusion as we felt a push from astern, while forward the boat seemed to strike a ledge. The sail collapsed and something rolled and tumbled like an earthquake beneath us. The whole crew was tossed into the stormy water. Storm, whale, and harpoon all blended together; and the whale, only scratched by the harpoon, escaped.

The boat, though full of water, was unharmed. We climbed back into it and sat up to our knees in seawater. The wind increased to a howl; we could not see the other boats. Around us the storm roared and crackled. Wet and cold, we sat thus until dawn. Then, at last, the *Pequod* loomed into view. The other boats had returned to the ship in good time; we were the last to be brought on board.

"Queequeg," said I, when they dragged me to the deck, "does this sort of thing happen often?" Without much

emotion, he gave me to understand that such things did often happen.

"Mr. Stubb," said I, turning to him, "I have heard you say that Mr. Starbuck is the most careful whaleman you have ever met. I suppose that going plump on a flying whale in a storm with your sail set is the height of carefulness?"

"Certain. I've lowered for whales from a leaking ship in a gale off Cape Horn."

Thinking of these things, I thought I might as well go below and make my will. After that I felt easier. Now, thought I, rolling up my sleeves, here goes for a cool, collected dive at death and destruction.

The *Pequod* made her way slowly north-east towards the island of Java. One still blue morning, when the waves whispered softly as they ran on, a strange sight was seen by the mast-head.

In the distance a great white mass lazily rose. It gleamed before us like a snow-slide. Then it sank, and rose once more. Was it Moby Dick? The mast-head cried out, "There! There she breaches! The White Whale!"

Bare-headed in the hot sun, Ahab stood forward and looked out at the white mass. Instantly he gave orders for lowering.

All four boats were soon on the water pulling towards their prey. It went down again, and then rose once more. Forgetting for the moment all thoughts of Moby Dick, we stared at the most wonderful thing that the seas had yet shown us. A vast mass, hundreds of yards in length and width, of a cream color, lay floating on the water. Long arms spread out from its center, curling and twisting like a nest of snakes. It had no face or front, but floated on the waves like a formless vision of life.

It slowly sank again. Starbuck exclaimed in a wild voice — "Almost rather had I seen Moby Dick and fought him, than to have seen thee, thou white ghost!"

"What was it, sir?" asked Flask.

"The great squid, which, they say, few whale boats ever saw and returned to their ports to tell of it."

But Ahab said nothing. Turning his boat, he sailed back to the *Pequod*, the rest following.

If to Starbuck the squid was a dreaded sight, to Queequeg it was quite different.

"When you see him 'quid," he said, "then you quick see him sperm whale."

The next day was very still. It was my turn at one of the mast-heads, and I swayed drowsily in the slow air. My eyes closed.

Suddenly, bubbles seemed to burst beneath my closed eyes, and I came back to life. And lo! not two hundred feet off, a gigantic sperm whale lay rolling in the water. Voices from all parts of the vessel shouted with mine as the great fish spouted into the air.

"Clear away the boats!" cried Ahab. Soon we glided in chase of the huge whale. He flitted his tail forty feet into the air, and then sank out of sight like a tower swallowed up.

We waited; and in a few minutes the whale rose again, close to Stubb's boat. Oars came into play, and Stubb cheered on his crew to the fight. The men tugged and strained at the oars, and the harpooneer stood up. The harpoon was hurled; something went hot and hissing along every one of their wrists. It was the rope attached to the harpoon. The rope spun across the wood of the boat so fast that a thin blue smoke rose up from it. The men wet it with seawater, and at last it held its place. Now the whale began to pull the boat along, so fast that the water seemed to boil around it. Each man held on to his seat so as not to be tossed to the foam. Whole Atlantics and Pacifics seemed to pass by as they shot on their way, till at last the whale slowed.

"Haul in!" cried Stubb, and all hands began to pull the boat up to the whale. Soon we were by his side, and Stubb threw dart after dart into him. The monster rolled and

churned in the water, blood running down his sides, and spouted jets of white vapor into the air. At last his agonized motion stopped.

"He's dead, Mr. Stubb," said the harpooneer.

Stubb's whale had been killed some distance from the ship. It was calm, and so three boats began the slow business of towing the whale to the *Pequod*. We rowed hour after hour to move that huge form, until darkness came on and we headed towards the lights of the ship. Finally the body was chained to the ship, later to be cut up and the parts stowed away for their various uses. You would think Ahab, as a whaling captain, would be glad to have it so. And yet some impatience, or despair, seemed to be working in him. It was as if the sight of that dead body reminded him of Moby Dick, yet to be killed.

CHAPTER FIVE

And so we traveled, following the whale. From time to time we would meet another ship, and Ahab would call across the water to ask if any aboard had seen the White Whale. One Englishman, aboard the *Samuel Enderby*, had met the whale the previous year; and he had a hook in place of a hand to show for it. When last seen, he told Ahab, the whale was heading east.

It was about this time that my poor friend Queequeg was taken with a fever. He grew thinner and thinner, until little seemed left of him but his frame and tattooing. The whole crew gave him up; and Queequeg himself showed his mind by a strange favor he asked. He asked the carpenter to build him a coffin in the shape of a canoe, like the ones in his native land. And so the carpenter measured him and built the coffin from some dark planking.

"Ah! Poor fellow! He'll have to die now," said a sailor.

But now that he had made every preparation for death, he suddenly came around. Soon there seemed no need of the coffin. When asked about his recovery, Queequeg said he had just remembered a little duty ashore, which he was leaving undone. Therefore he could not die yet — for to live or die, he said, was a matter of his own will. In a few days he was strong again, and using his coffin for a clothes-chest.

Thus occupied, we glided into the south seas of the Pacific. The ship's blacksmith stayed out on deck as he worked on bent harpoons. One day Captain Ahab came up to him with a bag full of steel nails and razors.

"I want a harpoon made," he said. "Something that will stick in a whale like his own bone."

And so the blacksmith made a harpoon out of that hard metal, with Ahab looking on. When he was ready to dip the blade into water to cool it, Ahab stopped him. Instead he called to him his three harpooneers.

"What say ye?" he cried. "Will ye give me as much blood as will cover this blade?" They nodded, and three cuts were made in their flesh to cool the whale's blade.

The warmest seas hide the worst storms. So it was that in the gentle Japanese seas we met the most dreaded of all storms, the typhoon. It burst from out of a cloudless sky like a bomb on a sleepy town.

By evening the *Pequod* was torn of her sails. When darkness came on, sky and sea roared and split with thunder, and blazed with lightning. The crew was on deck, tying down the boats and repairing what they could. Starbuck and Stubb directed the men; Stubb was singing:

Oh! jolly is the gale,
And a joker is the whale,
A-flourishin' his tail —
Such a funny, sporty, gamy, jesty, joky, hoky-poky lad, is
the Ocean, oh!

"Hold, Stubb," cried Starbuck. "Let the typhoon sing. If thou art a brave man thou wilt hold thy peace."

"But I am not a brave man, I am a coward. I sing to keep up my spirits, Mr. Starbuck."

"Madman! Look through my eyes if thou hast none of thy own." Starbuck turned Stubb toward the bow. "Do you not see that this storm comes from the east, the very course Ahab is to run for Moby Dick?"

"I don't understand ye. What's in the wind?"

"The storm that now hammers at us, we can turn into a fair wind to drive us home. Yonder, all is blackness of doom, but homeward, the sky lightens."

At that moment he heard a voice by his side.

"Who's there?"

"Old Thunder!" said Ahab, groping his way along the deck. Suddenly his path was made plain to him by a flickering light.

"Look aloft!" cried Starbuck. "The St. Elmo's lights! The corposants!"

All the yard-arms were tipped with a pale fire. The St. Elmo's lights, or corposants, are pale flames that appear around the masts and spars of ships in stormy weather. Each of the masts was silently burning in that stormy air, like three tall candles.

The men of the crew were silent. They stood together, staring up at the lights, their eyes gleaming in that pale light.

"The corposants have mercy on us all!" cried Stubb.

"Aye, aye, men!" cried Ahab. "Look up at it; the white flame but lights the way to the White Whale!"

"The boat!" cried Starbuck. "Look at thy boat, old man!"

Ahab's harpoon had been tied to his boat's bow; from its keen steel blade there now came a flame of pale fire. As the harpoon burned there like a serpent's tongue, Starbuck grasped Ahab by the arm.

"God is against thee, old man! 'Tis an ill voyage! Let me set the sails, while we may, and make a fair wind of it homewards."

Hearing Starbuck, the frightened crew ran to the masts, as if to set sail. But Ahab snatched up the burning harpoon and waved it like a torch among them.

"All your oaths to hunt the White Whale are as binding as mine," he said. "And heart, soul, body, and life, old Ahab is bound. Look ye here; thus I blow out the last fear!" And with one breath he blew out the flame.

The storm blew itself out. The next day a large ship, the *Rachel*, was seen bearing down on the *Pequod*. As she came near, Ahab's voice was heard.

"Hast seen the White Whale?"

"Aye, yesterday. Have ye seen a whaleboat adrift?"

Holding down his joy, Ahab said no to this question. The captain of the other boat was then seen lowering himself down her side, and soon sprang onto the deck of the *Pequod*. Ahab recognized him as a fellow Nantucketer.

"Where did you see him?" cried Ahab. "How was it?"

It seemed that the previous day, they had sighted the white hump of Moby Dick. Three of the whale boats were already out a-whaling; a fourth was lowered for the White Whale. This fourth boat seemed to have struck the whale; then it was towed into the distance. It grew dark — the other boats were picked up — and still no sign of the fourth boat. The *Rachel* had sailed all night without finding it.

Her captain wanted the *Pequod* to join his search for the missing boat.

"My boy, my own boy is among them," exclaimed the captain. "For forty-eight hours let me use your ship. I will gladly pay for it. I will not go till you say aye to me. Yes, yes, I see that you soften — run, run, men, run, and stand by to set sail."

"Stop!" cried Ahab. "Touch not a rope. Captain Gardiner, I will not do it. Even now I lose time. Good-bye. God bless ye, man, and may I forgive myself, but I must go."

Turning his face away, Ahab hurried below. The other captain silently returned to his ship.

CHAPTER SIX

It was a clear steel-blue day. Ahab leaned over the side, and watched his shadow in the water. Starbuck drew near to him. Ahab turned.

"Oh, Starbuck! It is a mild wind, and a mild sky. On such a day I struck my first whale — a boy-harpooneer of eighteen. Forty years ago! Yes, and of those forty years I have not spent three ashore. When I think of the life I have led, what a forty-years fool old Ahab seems! I feel so old, Starbuck, faint, and bowed, and humped, as if I were Adam walking through the centuries since Paradise. Stay on board, Starbuck! Lower not when Ahab gives chase to Moby Dick."

"Oh, my captain! Noble soul!" replied Starbuck. "Let us fly these deadly waters. I think, sir, they have such mild blue days, even as this, in Nantucket."

But Ahab turned his face away, and crossed to the other side to stare out over the water.

That night a strange smell, sometimes given forth by the sperm whale, was smelled by the crew. Ahab ordered the ship to follow that smell, and sent all hands aloft. At day break he joined them at the mast-heads, and then raised a cry: "There she blows! A hump like a snow-hill! It is Moby Dick!"

The whale was a mile or so ahead, rolling with the waves.

"Lower the boats, Mr. Starbuck, but remember, you stay on board."

Soon the boats sped through the sea. The hunters came close to their prey, so that his entire sparkling hump could be seen, sliding along the sea. Before it went a white shadow from the broad, milky forehead. A gentle joyousness seemed to be in the gliding whale, so gracefully did he swim. Soon the fore part of him rose from the water, and his body formed a high arch in the air. Then, waving his tail, he went out of sight. The boats waited, floating.

Suddenly, as Ahab looked down into the depths, he saw a white living spot that rose and grew with a wonderful speed. It turned and revealed two crooked, glistening rows of teeth. It was Moby Dick's open mouth and jaw, yawning beneath the boat like an open tomb. Ahab tried to turn the boat, but too late; the whale caught it up in his mouth and shook it, as a cat will shake a mouse.

Ahab and the crew fell into the sea, and the White Whale circled about them. The other boats dared not come closer. Then the *Pequod* approached, and drove the whale off; and Ahab and his crew were pulled to safety.

The *Pequod* set full sail, and chased the wake of the whale through the night. The next day, Moby Dick was seen, springing out of the sea. The boats were lowered again.

As if to strike quick terror into them, Moby Dick turned, and was now coming for the three crews. He rushed among them, heedless of the harpoons darted at him from every boat. He lashed his tail, and crossed and recrossed, and tangled up the ropes attached to him. Ahab cut his ropes; but the boats of Stubb and Flask were dragged together and crushed. Then the whale disappeared into the sea.

While the two crews were paddling about in the water, Ahab's boat seemed suddenly drawn up to heaven, as if by

unseen wires. The White Whale had dashed his broad forehead against its bottom and sent it, turning over and over, into the air. It fell upside-down, and Ahab and his men struggled out from under it. Then the whale swam slowly off, trailing after him the tangled lines.

"Great God!" cried Starbuck, when Ahab was back on deck. "Never wilt thou capture him, old man! Two days chased; twice broken to splinters; what more would you have? Shall we be towed by this whale to the infernal world? Oh, blasphemy to hunt him more!"

"This is all but fate, man," said Ahab. "Tomorrow Moby Dick will spout his last."

And so into the third day we followed the whale. Hours passed — time itself seemed to hold its breath. And then voices cried out from the three mast-heads.

The boats were lowered; Ahab paused beside his chief mate.

"Starbuck!" he said. "Some men die at low tide; some at full flood. I feel like a wave that's all come to a peak. Shake hands with me, man."

Their hands met, and Starbuck's eyes filled with tears.

The three boats returned to their chase. The whale could not be seen. Then, a rumbling sound was heard, and a vast form, covered with harpoons and ropes, shot from the sea.

"Give way!" cried Ahab to the oarsmen, and the boat sped forward. But Moby Dick seemed enraged. He came churning his tail between the boats, smashing the bows of two of them, but leaving Ahab's boat unharmed. He kept swimming, seeming to follow a straight path out to sea.

"Oh, Ahab," cried Starbuck aboard the *Pequod*, "it is not too late to stop. See! Moby Dick does not seek thee. It is thou that madly seekest him!"

The crews of the other boats returned to the *Pequod* for repairs; but Ahab followed the White Whale. The whale slowed, and Ahab drew along his side and threw a harpoon into the hated whale. Moby Dick flung himself

sideways, tilting the boat and throwing one of the oarsmen into the sea. In turning, the whale caught sight of the *Pequod*. Perhaps he thought it another enemy, for he bore down upon its advancing bow.

"The ship! The ship!" cried Ahab. His men strained at the oars, but at that moment two planks burst through in the whale boat, and it began to sink.

All eyes aboard the *Pequod* were on Moby Dick. Revenge and evil seemed to live in his form. In spite of all they could do, his broad white forehead struck the bow, throwing the crew to the deck. They heard water pour through the hole. The whale swam under the ship and came to rest near Ahab's boat.

"For hate's sake I stab at thee," cried Ahab. "*Thus*, I give up the spear!" He threw his harpoon, and the whale flew forward, towing the harpoon-rope. The rope caught on something; Ahab bent to clear it; he did clear it; but a flying loop of the rope caught him around the neck. Silently he was shot out of the boat, and the rope-end flew after him and disappeared into the sea.

His oarsmen stood still; then — "The ship! Where is the ship!" For only the sinking masts of the *Pequod* could be seen above the water. Turning slowly, it seemed to be caught in a whirlpool. Ahab's boat was caught up in that same whirlpool, and the ship and boat and men spun around and vanished from sight. Screaming birds flew over the spot, and the great shroud of the sea rolled on as it rolled five thousand years ago.

Only one survived the wreck. I was Ahab's oarsman who was tossed from his boat; I alone was not drawn into the whirlpool. From the center of that whirlpool, something burst out of the sea and fell at my side. It was Queequeg's coffin. Held up by that coffin, I floated for a day and night. On the second day, a sail drew near and picked me up at last. It was the *Rachel*, that in her search for her missing children, found only another orphan.

GLOSSARY

aft (aft)   near the back end of a ship

beam (bēm)   the middle or widest part of a ship

bulwarks (bul' werks)   the sides of a ship that form a
kind of wall around the upper deck

corposants   *see* St. Elmo's lights

harpoon (har poon')   a spear used in hunting large
fish or whales

harpooneer (har poon ēr')   a person who uses a
harpoon to hunt with

lee (lē)   the side of a ship that is sheltered from the
wind

prey (prā)   an animal that is hunted for food

St. Elmo's lights (sānt el' mōz līts')   flaming lights
that are sometimes seen in stormy weather

schooner (skoo' nər)   a ship with two masts, the
smaller mast in front

tiller (til' ər)   a lever that is used to steer a boat